Benjamin Bear
Says Sorry

CANDLE
BOOKS

Published in 2006 by Candle Books
(a publishing imprint of Lion Hudson plc).

Distributed in the UK by Marston Book Services Ltd,
PO Box 269, Abingdon, Oxon OX14 4YN
Distributed in the USA by Kregel Publications,
Grand Rapids, Michigan 49501

Worldwide co-edition produced by Lion Hudson plc,
Mayfield House, 256 Banbury Road,
Oxford OX2 7DH England
Tel:+44 (o) 1865 302750   Fax: +44 (o) 1865 302757
email:coed@lionhudson.com   www.lionhudson.com

UK   ISBN-13: 978-185985-632-1
        ISBN-10: 1-85985-632-2
USA ISBN-13: 978-0-8254-7325-8
        ISBN-10: 0-8254-7325-X

Printed in China

Benjamin Bear

Says Sorry

Claire Freedman

Illustrated by Steve Smallman

The sun shone brightly. Bees buzzed happily.
And little Benjamin Bear felt full of bounce!

"Hooray!" he cried,
skipping down the hill.
"This is my favourite kind
of day for having fun."

Down by the stream, Benjamin's friend Snippy was doing a bit of fishing.

"That looks fun!" Benjamin cried, rushing across. "Can I try?"

Snippy handed over his fishing rod.
"Careful, Benjamin!" he cried. "Mind
where you're swinging it!"

Oh no! Benjamin accidentally sent
Snippy's hat flying into the stream!

"Whoops!" Benjamin gasped. "How did that happen? I'd better have fun doing something else." And he hurried off.

"Huh!" sighed Snippy, wading into the water to fetch his hat. "It would have been nice if Benjamin had said sorry!"

Further down stream, Benjamin found his friend Lofty building sand pies.

"Oooh, that's fun!" Benjamin said. "Can I help?"

"Of course, Benjamin," Lofty replied.

Benjamin started digging excitedly.
Sand flew everywhere!

"Hey, watch out!" cried Lofty. "You're
sending that my way!"

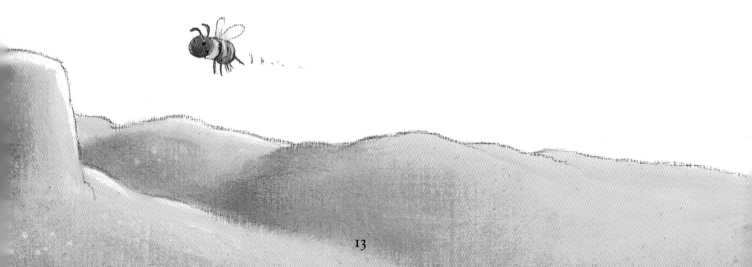

"Whoops!" Benjamin said. "I forgot you were behind me, Lofty. I'll go and have fun somewhere else."

Away he scampered.

"Huh!" sighed Lofty, brushing himself down. "It would have been nice if Benjamin had said sorry!"

Benjamin decided to find a big tree to climb. That was fun too! He clambered up through the branches of a huge oak tree.

"Oh look!" he giggled. "There's Stripe down there. I know – I'll give him a funny surprise!"

Benjamin popped his head out through the leaves.
"BOO!" he shouted at the top of his voice.

"Help!" gasped Stripe, leaping up with a start. "Oh
Benjamin – you gave me a scare. I was fast asleep!"

"Whoops, I thought you were awake!" Benjamin said. He jumped down and rushed off.

"Huh!" sighed Stripe. "It would have been nice if Benjamin had said sorry!"

Benjamin whistled cheerfully as he bounced along. Sniff, sniff! He could smell something delicious – strawberry bushes!

"Yummy!" he said. "I'll pick some strawberries for tea."

Soon Benjamin had gathered a nice little pile of fruit.
He sat down for a rest when... *Ding-a-ling!* Someone
came whizzing along on their tricycle.

"Mind my strawberries!" Benjamin shouted.

Too late! The cyclist rode right over them!

"Huh!" said Benjamin crossly. "I know that was an accident. But it would have been nice if he'd said sorry!"

Suddenly Benjamin thought. "Oh dear!" he gulped. "I never said sorry to Snippy or Lofty or Stripe – did I? I upset *them* by accident too."

But it wasn't too late to put
that right. Benjamin quickly
picked more strawberries, and
raced back to find his friends.

"I'm sorry!" he told them.

"That's alright, Benjamin," his friends answered, looking much happier. "We know you didn't mean it."

"Hooray!" cried Benjamin. Suddenly he felt full of bounce again!

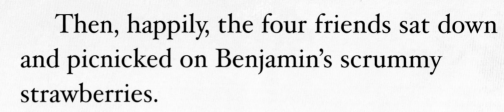

Then, happily, the four friends sat down and picnicked on Benjamin's scrummy strawberries.

And together they watched the sun go down on a lovely summer's day.

Benjamin Bear decided that having good friends really *was* the best fun of all!

Everybody does things wrong,
We all can make mistakes.
It's easy though, to put things right,
"I'm sorry" is all it takes.